Thomas Love Peacock

Gl' Ingannati - the Deceived

a comedy performed at Siena in 1531 - and Aelia Laelia Crispis

Thomas Love Peacock

Gl' Ingannati - the Deceived
a comedy performed at Siena in 1531 - and Aelia Laelia Crispis

ISBN/EAN: 9783337383688

Printed in Europe, USA, Canada, Australia, Japan

Cover: Foto ©Andreas Hilbeck / pixelio.de

More available books at **www.hansebooks.com**

GL' INGANNATI.

THE DECEIVED:

𝔄 Comedy

PERFORMED AT SIENA IN 1531:

AND

AELIA LAELIA CRISPIS.

BY

T. L. PEACOCK.

LONDON:

CHAPMAN AND HALL, 193 PICCADILLY.

1862.

PREFACE.

MR. COLLIER, in his *Annals of the Stage*,* published in 1831, gives an account of a Diary, in which he found recorded a performance of Shakspeare's *Twelfth Night*. " This Diary," he says, " I was fortunate enough to meet with among the Harleian MSS. in the Museum. It was kept by an individual, whose name is nowhere given, but who seems to have been a barrister, and consequently a member of one of the Inns of Court. The dates, which are inserted with much particularity, extend from January, 1600-1, to April, 1603 : and when I state, that it includes original and unpublished anecdotes of Shakspeare, Spenser, Tarleton, Ben Jonson, Marston, Sir John Davis, Sir Walter Raleigh, and others, it will not be disputed that it is a very valuable and remarkable source of information. . . . .

" The period when Shakspeare wrote his *Twelfth Night, or What you Will,* has been much disputed among the commentators. Tyrwhitt was inclined to fix it in 1614, and Malone was for some years

* Vol. i., pages 327, 328.

of the same opinion : but he afterwards changed the date he had adopted to 1607. Chalmers thought he found circumstances in the play to justify him in naming 1613 ; but what I am about to state affords a striking, and, at the same time, a rarely occurring and convincing proof, how little these conjectures merit confidence. That comedy was unquestionably written before 1602, for in February of that year it was an established play, and so much liked, that it was chosen for performance, at the Reader's Feast on Candlemas day, at the Inn of Court to which the author of this Diary belonged — most likely the Middle Temple, which, at that date, was famous for its costly entertainments. After reading the following quotation, it is utterly impossible, although the name of the poet be not mentioned, to feel a moment's doubt as to the identity of the play there described and the production of Shakspeare :—

" ' Feb. 2, 1601-2.

" ' At our feast we had a play called Twelve Night, or What you Will, much like the Comedy of Errors, or Menechmi in Plautus, but most like and neere to that in Italian called *Inganni*. A good practice in it, to make the steward believe his lady widdowe * was in love with him, by counterfayting a letter, as from his lady, in general termes, telling him what she liked best in him, and prescribing his gestures, inscribing his apparaile. &c., and then, when he came to practise, making him believe they took him to be mad.'

" Should the Italian comedy, called *Inganni*, turn

---

* Olivia is not a widow ; but the misprision is of no moment.

up, we shall probably find in it the actual original of Twelfth Night, which it has been hitherto supposed was founded upon the story of Apollonius and Silla, in Barnabe Riche's Farewell to Military Profession, twice printed, viz.: in 1583 and 1606."

Riche's Farewell was reprinted by the Shakspeare Society in 1846. The editor, after alluding to Bandello's tale of Nicuola and Lattantio, and Belleforest's French version of that tale, says: "It seems more likely that Riche resorted to Bandello; but it is possible that this novel was one of those which had been dramatized before Riche wrote, and if this were the case, it would establish the new and important fact, that a play on the same story as Twelfth Night, had been produced before 1581.

"Two Italian comedies, upon very similar incidents, one called *Inganni*, and the other *Ingannati*, were certainly then in existence, and may have formed the groundwork of a drama, anterior to Shakspeare, in our own language. The names given by Riche to the various personages are not those which occur in Bandello, Belleforest, or the Italian comedies: neither are they the same as any used by Shakspeare. Riche perhaps obtained them from the old English drama."

If a play on the same subject as Twelfth Night had been produced before 1581, it could scarcely have escaped the notice of the writer of the Diary. As to the two comedies, *Gl' Inganni* and *Gl' Ingannati*, the latter was first in time, and claims to be strictly original.

The *Ingannati* was performed in Siena in 1531; the *Inganni* at Milan in 1547.* The first has most re-

* *Gl' Inganni, Comedia del Signor N. S. [Sechi], recitata in*

semblance to *Twelfth Night*, and was probably in the mind of the author of the Diary, though he called it *Inganni*. That he could make a slight mistake as to what was before him, is evident from his calling Olivia a widow.

I first became acquainted with the *Inganni* in the French version of Pierre de Larivey, under the title of *Les Tromperies*, 1611. This French comedy had become very scarce; but it has been republished in the *Ancien Théâtre Français* of the *Bibliothèque Elzévirienne.** I have since read the original in the British Museum.

The scene of the *Inganni* was laid in Italy. Larivey transferred it to France. I give the Italian argument.

Anselmo, a merchant of Genoa, who traded with the Levant, went on a voyage to Syria, taking with him his wife and his twin children, Fortunato and Ginevra, aged four years, whom, for the convenience

---

Milano l' anno 1547, *dinanzi alla Maestà del Re Filippo. In Fiorenza, appresso i Giunti,* 1562.*

Charles V., before leaving Spain in 1543, had given the title of king of Spain to his son Philip (Philip II.)

* The comedies of Larivey, nine in number, all taken from the Italian, are all reprinted in this collection. *Les Tromperies* is the ninth. The editor, M. Viollet Le Duc, says: "Les six premières comédies de Larivey obtinrent un grand succès, constaté par plusieurs éditions. Les trois dernières n'ont été imprimées qu'une fois, ce qui s'explique par la mort de l'auteur, et surtout par cette circonstance, que ces trois pièces n'avoient pas, comme les premières, l'attrait de la nouveauté. Ce volume n'ayant eu qu'une seule édition, est devenue très rare, et se paie au poids de l'or dans les ventes publiques."—*Tome* v. p. xx.

---

* This is the oldest edition I have seen referred to. There are editions in the British Museum of 1566, 1582, 1587, 1602, 1615.

of the sea passage, he dressed precisely alike, so that
the girl passed for a boy. On the voyage, they were
captured by Corsairs. Anselmo was taken into Na-
tolia, where he remained in slavery fourteen years.
Fortunato was several times sold, but ultimately in
Naples, where the scene is laid, and where he is
serving Dorotea, a lady no better than she should
be. The mother and Ginevra, after various adven-
tures, were purchased, also in Naples, by Messer
Massimo Caraccioli. The mother had deemed it
prudent to continue the male apparel of her daughter,
and through her the brother and sister had been
made known to each other. The mother had died
six years previously to the opening of the comedy.
Ginevra had taken the name of Roberto. Massimo
has a son named Gostanzo, and a daughter named
Portia. Portia is in love with the supposed Roberto,
and Gostanzo with Dorotea, who returns his attach-
ment, but her mother, Gilletta, a rapacious and
tyrannical woman, forbids him the house, after she
has extorted from him all the money he could dis-
pose of. Ginevra, persecuted by the love of Portia,
smuggles her brother Fortunato into the house, and,
when occasion serves, substitutes him for herself.
At the opening of the play, Portia is on the point
of increasing the population of Naples. Ginevra is
in double grief, fearing the anger of Massimo, and
suffering under her own love for Gostanzo, seeing
his love for Dorotea. In despair, she discovers herself to Gostanzo, who transfers his love to her, and
Anselmo arrives, abundantly rich, in time to appease
the wrath of Massimo, and unite Gostanzo to Ginevra,
and Fortunato to Portia.

In all this, what little there is of resemblance
to Twelfth Night, is taken, as will be presently
seen, and not changed for the better, from the *Ingannati.*

Much of this comedy is borrowed, in parts closely
translated, from the *Asinaria* of Plautus. Cleaereta,
the mother; Philenium, the daughter; Argyrippus,
the lover; are reproduced in Gilletta, Dorotea, and
Gostanzo. So are the old physician and his wife
reproductions of the old man Demaenetus, and his
wife Artemona. The scenes of the *Asinaria,* between
Cleaereta and Argyrippus, *Act* i., *Scene* 3; Cleaereta
and Philenium, *Act* iii., *Scene* 1; the portion of *Act*
iii., *Scene* 3, which is between Argyrippus and Philenium; the concluding scene, in which Artemona
carries off Demaenetus from the house of Cleaereta,
Act v., *Scene* 2; are copied in the *Inganni*, in the
scenes between Gostanzo and Gilletta, *Act* i., *Scene* 1;
between Gilletta and Dorotea, *Act* ii., *Scene* 2; between
Gostanzo and Dorotea, *Act* ii., *Scene* 5; and in the
concluding scene, in which the physician's wife
carries off her husband from the house of Gilletta,
Act v., *Scene* 10.

There is also a captain of the Bobadil order, who
is imposed on and fleeced by Gilletta and Dorotea,
and afterwards, finding the house barred against
him, besieges it, as Terence's Thraso does the house
of Thais,* and is as easily repulsed. There are

---

* *Thraso.* Hancine ego ut contumeliam tam insignem in me
　　　　accipiam, Gnatho?
Mori me satius est. Simalio, Donax, Syrisce, sequimini.
Primum aedeis expugnabo.—*Eunuchus, Actus* iv., *Scena* 7.
　Le Capitaine. Ha ciel! qu'il me faille endurer un tel affront!
. . . . . Allons chercher le capitaine Tailbras, le capitaine

other gatherings from the Latin drama. The comedy, in short, though very entertaining, has no originality.

It seems strange that the *Inganni* should have remained undiscovered by Shakspearian critics: but the cause which concealed the *Ingannati* from their researches, is somewhat curious. It appears with the title *Comedia del Sacrificio degli Intronati.* The *Sacrificio* is a series of songs to music, in which various characters, who have suffered from "the pangs of despised love," renounce love, and each in succession sacrifices on an altar some gift or memorial of his unkind or faithless mistress. This prelude, which has no relation whatever to the comedy, being concluded, the comedy follows, with its own proper title *Gl' Ingannati.*

There are many editions of this comedy. The earliest of which I have yet found a record, is of 1537. It is not probable that this was the first. There were others of 1538, 1550, 1554, 1562, 1563, 1569, 1585. Four of these are in the British Museum; and one, *In Venetia,* without date. And it was included in collections; one, containing all the comedies of the Intronati, 1611; another, with four other comedies and notes by Ruscelli, which I find mentioned without the date. The title of an edition in my possession, is, *Comedia del Sacrificio de gli Intronati, Celebrato ne i giuochi d' un Carnovale in*

Brisecuisse, Brafort, Cachemaille, Pinçargent, Grippetout, et mes autres amis; puis retournons faire bravade à ces poltronnes. —*Les Tromperies, Acte* iv., *Scène* 2. This version is better than the corresponding Italian.

Siena, l'Anno MDXXXI. Sotto il Sodo,* dignissimo Archintronato. Di nuovo corretta e ristampata. In Venetia, appresso Francesco Rampazetto, MDLXII.†

Gl' Intronati, the Thunder-stricken, was an Academy in Siena, which distinguished itself at that period by dramatic productions. The Italian Academies gave themselves fantastical names, *I Caliginosi, I Dubbiosi, I Chimerici : The Dark, the Doubtful, the Chimerical*, and so forth. Their members assumed conformable appellations. *L' Amor Costante*, a comedy performed at Siena, before the Emperor Charles V., in 1536,‡ is given in the title as by *Signor Stordito*,§ *Intronato : Master Stunned of the Thunder-stricken*. This comedy is introduced by a dialogue, between the Prologue and a Spaniard, in the course of which the Spaniard inquires—

Who is the author of the comedy? Is it the most divine Pietro Aretino? ‖

Prologue. The author is a member of an academy, which has been in Siena many years.

Spaniard. What is the name of this academy?

Prologue. The academy of the *Intronati*.

Spaniard. The *Intronati?* The fame of this academy has

---

* Marcantonio Piccolomini.

† There was a French translation of *Gl' Ingannati*, under the title of *Les Abusez*, by Charles Estienne ; of which there appear to have been three editions : Lyon, 1543 ; Paris, 1549 and 1558.

‡ In a Venetian reprint before me, the date of the first performance is given as 1531 ; but the play has many historical indications which determine the time. One will suffice. The action passes in the pontificate of Paul III., and two years after the death of Clement VII., who died in 1534.

§ Alessandro Piccolomini.

‖ Pietro Aretino had produced two of his five comedies before 1536.

spread through all parts of Spain; and its name has gone so far, that it has reached the ears of the emperor. How rejoiced should I be if I could belong to this academy! And if you would have me bound to you for the whole time of my life, place me among you.

Prologue. If you are disposed to observe our rules, I will gladly exert myself on your behalf.

Spaniard. What are the rules?

Prologue. Few and simple. To seek knowledge and wisdom: to take the world as it comes: to be the affectionate and devoted slave of these ladies:* and, for the love of them, to make now and then a comedy, or some other work, to show our implicit submission.

Spaniard. These rules are greatly to my mind; and if I can obtain the favour of being placed in the academy, I will most faithfully observe them all.

Renouard, in the *Bibliothèque d'un Amateur* (*Paris*, 1819, *tome* iii., *pp.* 109—119), gives a list of Italian dramas in his possession, which he introduces with the following notice :—

" Le XVIe siècle produisit une multitude innombrable de pièces dramatiques italiennes, qui actuellement se lisent peu : beaucoup d'entre elles continuent cependant à être recherchées des Italiens, soit pour la pureté du style, qualité par laquelle beaucoup se distinguent, soit même pour leur bizarrerie, et

---

* The *Intronati* were especially devoted to the service of the ladies. The Prologue of the *Ingannati* addresses the ladies only. *Io vi veggio fin di quà,* NOBILISSIME DONNE, *meravigliare di vedermivi così dinanzi, in questo habito, ed insieme di questo apparecchio, come se noi havessimo a fare qualche comedia.*

I see you, even from hence, MOST NOBLE LADIES, *wonder at seeing me thus before you, in this dress, and also at these preparations, as if we were about to produce some comedy.*

The prologues of other comedies of the period address the spectators generally.

souvent pour la seule rareté des exemplaires. Ne voulant point ici faire collection de ce genre de pièces, on a seulement choisi parmi celles que l'on a crues recommandables par aucune de ces diverses causes, et l'on n'a admis aucun exemplaire qui ne soit de parfaite conservation."

The list of dramas includes twenty comedies of the sixteenth century; two of which are the *Ingannati* and *Inganni*, the former with the usual title page, *Comedia del Sacrificio*, without date. The *Inganni* is given as *nuovamente ristampata. In Fiorenza*, 1568.

To return to the *Ingannati*. The Prologue says: "The fable is new : never before seen nor read : nor drawn from any other source than the industrious brains of the Academicians of the *Intronati*."

This, therefore, we may fairly assume to be the original source, from which all other versions of the elements of the story are drawn ; the elements being these :

A girl assumes male apparel, and enters as a page into the service of a man, with whom she either previously is, or subsequently becomes, in love. He employs her as a messenger to a lady, who will not listen to his suit. The lady falls in love with the supposed page, and, under the influence of a mistake, marries the girl's twin brother. The lover transfers his affection to the damsel, who has served him in disguise.

I propose to translate the scenes in which these four characters are principally concerned, and to give a connecting outline of the rest.

The original has no stage directions, and the scenes have no indication of place. I have inserted some stage directions, and have indicated the places of the action, on what appeared to me probable grounds.

The house of Virginio is too far from the house of Gherardo, to be shown in the same street. This is apparent from several passages, especially from *Act* iv., *Scene* 7, where Virginio asks Gherardo to take in his supposed daughter, because he cannot take her to his own house without her being seen in male apparel by all the city.

The house of Gherardo is near the hotels.

The house of Flaminio is in a distinct locality from both. It is clearly not under observation from either.

I have, therefore, marked three changes of scene:

A street, with two hotels, and the house of Gherardo.

A street, with the house of Flaminio.

A street, with the house of Virginio.

THE DECEIVED.

DRAMATIS PERSONÆ.

GHERARDO FOIANI, *an old man, father of Isabella.*
VIRGINIO BELLENZINI, *an old man, father of Lelia and Fabrizio.*
FLAMINIO DE' CARANDINI, *in love with Isabella.*
FABRIZIO, *son of Virginio.*
MESSER PIERO, *a pedant, tutor of Fabrizio.*
L' AGIATO, ⎫
FRUELLA, ⎬ *rival hotel-keepers.*
GIGLIO, *a Spaniard.*
SPELA, *servant of Gherardo.*
SCATIZZA, *servant of Virginio.*
CRIVELLO, *servant of Flaminio.*
STRAGUALCIA, *servant of Fabrizio.*

LELIA, *daughter of Virginio, disguised as a page, under the name of Fabio.*
ISABELLA, *daughter of Gherardo.*
CLEMENTIA, *nurse of Lelia.*
PASQUELLA, *housekeeper to Gherardo.*
CITTINA, *a girl, daughter of Clementia.*

The SCENE *is in* MODENA.

THE DECEIVED.

ACT I.

SCENE I.—*A Street, with the house of* Virginio.

Virginio *and* Gherardo.

Virginio is an old merchant, who has two children, a son and a daughter, Fabrizio and Lelia. He has lost his property and his son in the sack of Rome, May 1527, when his daughter had just finished her thirteenth year. The comedy being performed in the Carnival of 1531, the girl is in her seventeenth year. Another old man, Gherardo, who is wealthy, wishes to marry her, and the father assents, provided the maiden is willing. Gherardo thinks that the father's will ought to be sufficient, and that it only rests with him to make his daughter do as he pleases.

SCENE II.

Virginio *and* Clementia.

Virginio, having shortly before gone on business to Bologna, in company with a Messer Buonaparte and others, had left Lelia in a convent with her Aunt Camilla, and now, in the intention of her

c

marriage, desires Lelia's nurse, Clementia, to go to the convent to bring her home. Clementia must first go to mass.

SCENE III.—*A Street, with the house of* FLAMINIO.

LELIA, *afterwards* CLEMENTIA.

Lelia (in male apparel). It is a great boldness in me, that, knowing the licentious customs of these wild youths of Modena, I should venture abroad alone at this early hour. What would become of me, if any one of them should suspect my sex? But the cause is my love for the cruel and ungrateful Flaminio. Oh, what a fate is mine! I love one who hates me. I serve one who does not know me: and, for more bitter grief, I aid him in his love for another, without any other hope than that of satiating my eyes with his sight. Thus far all has gone well: but now, how can I do? My father has returned. Flaminio has come to live in the town. I can scarcely hope to continue here without being discovered: and if it should be so, my reputation will be blighted for ever, and I shall become the fable of the city. Therefore I have come forth at this hour to consult my nurse, whom, from the window, I have seen coming this way. But I will first see if she knows me in this dress. (*Clementia enters.*)

Clementia. In good faith, Flaminio must be returned to Modena: for I see his door open. Oh! if Lelia knew it, it would appear to her a thousand years till she came back to her father's house. But who is this young coxcomb that keeps crossing before me, backward and forward? What do you mean by it?

Take yourself off, or I will show you how I like such chaps.

Lelia. Good morning, good mother.

Clementia. I seem to know this boy. Tell me, where can I have seen you?

Lelia. You pretend not to know me, eh? Come a little nearer: nearer still: on this side. Now?

Clementia. Is it possible? Can you be Lelia? Oh, misery of my life! What can this mean, my child?

Lelia. Oh! if you cry out in this way, I must go.

Clementia. Is this the honour you do to your father, to your house, to yourself, to me, who have brought you up? Come in instantly. You shall not be seen in this dress.

Lelia. Pray have a little patience.

Clementia. Are you not ashamed to be seen so?

Lelia. Am I the first? I have seen women in Rome go in this way by hundreds.

Clementia. They must be no better than they should be.

Lelia. By no means.

Clementia. Why do you go so? Why have you left the convent? Oh! if your father knew it, he would kill you.

Lelia. He would end my affliction. Do you think I value life?

Clementia. But why do you go so? Tell me.

Lelia. Listen, and you shall hear. You will then know how great is my affliction, why I have left the convent, why I go thus attired, and what I wish you to do in the matter. But step more aside, lest any one should pass who may recognize me, seeing me talking with you.

Clementia. You destroy me with impatience.

Lelia. You know that after the miserable sack of Rome, my father, having lost everything, and with his property my brother Fabrizio, in order not to be alone in his house, took me from the service of the Signora Marchesana, with whom he had placed me, and, constrained by necessity, we returned to our house in Modena to live on the little that remained to us here. You know, also, that my father, having been considered a friend of the Count Guido Rangon,* was not well looked on by many.

Clementia. Why do you tell me what I know better than you? I know, too, for what reason you left the city, to live at our farm of Pontanile, and that I went with you.

Lelia. You know, also, how bitter were my feelings at that time : not only remote from all thoughts of love, but almost from all human thought, considering that, having been a captive among soldiers, I could not, however purely and becomingly I might live, escape malicious observations. And you know how often you scolded me for my melancholy, and exhorted me to lead a more cheerful life.

Clementia. If I know it, why do you tell it me? Go on.

Lelia. Because it is necessary to remind you of all this, that you may understand what follows. It happened at this time that Flaminio Carandini, from having been attached to the same party as ourselves, formed an intimate friendship with my father, came daily to our house, began to admire me secretly,

---

* This count makes a conspicuous figure in Guicciardini's History.

then took to sighing and casting down his eyes. By degrees I took increasing pleasure in his manners and conversation, not, however, even dreaming of love. But his continuous visits, and sighs, and signs of admiration at last made me aware that he was not a little taken with me, and I, who had never felt love before, deeming him worthy of my dearest thoughts, became in love with him so strongly that I had no longer any delight but in seeing him.

Clementia. Much of this I also knew.

Lelia. You know, too, that when the Spanish soldiers left Rome my father went there, to see if any of our property remained, but, still more, to see if he could learn any news of my brother. He sent me to Mirandola, to stay, till his return, with my Aunt Giovanna. With what grief I separated myself from my dear Flaminio you may well say, who so often dried my tears. I remained a year at Mirandola, and on my father's return I came back to Modena, more than ever enamoured of him who was my first love, and thinking still that he loved me as before.

Clementia. Oh, insanity ! How many Modenese have you found constant in the love of one for a year? One month to one, another month to another, is the extent of their devotion.

Lelia. I met him, and he scarcely remembered me, more than if he had never seen me. But the worst of it is, that he has set his heart on Isabella, the daughter of Gherardo Foiani, who is not only very beautiful, but the only child of her father, if the crazy old fellow does not marry again.

Clementia. He thinks himself certain of having you,

and says, that your father has promised you to him.
But all this does not explain to me why you have
left the convent, and go about in male apparel.

Lelia. The old fellow certainly shall not have me.
But my father, after his return from Rome, having
business at Bologna, placed me, as I would not return
to Mirandola, in the convent with my cousin Amabile
de' Cortesi. I found, that among these reverend
mothers and sisters, love was the principal subject of
conversation. I therefore felt emboldened to open my
heart to Amabile. She pitied me, and found means to
bring Flaminio, who was then living out of the town,
in a palazzo near the convent, several times to speak
with her and with others, where I, concealed behind
curtains, might feast my eyes with seeing him, and
my ears with hearing him. One day, I heard him la-
menting the death of a page, whose good service he
highly praised, saying how glad he should be if he
could find such another. It immediately occurred to
me, that I would try to supply the vacant place, and
consulting with Sister Amabile, she encouraged me,
instructed me how to proceed, and fitted me with some
new clothes, which she had had made, in order that
she might, as others do, go out in disguise about her
own affairs. So one morning early, I left the convent
in this attire, and went to Flaminio's palazzo. There
I waited till Flaminio came out : and Fortune be
praised, he no sooner saw me, than he asked me most
courteously, what I wanted, and whence I came.

Clementia. Is it possible that you did not fall dead
with shame ?

Lelia. Far from it, indeed. Love bore me up. I
answered frankly, that I was from Rome, and that

being poor, I was seeking service. He examined me several times from head to foot so earnestly, that I was almost afraid he would know me. He then said, that if I pleased to stay with him, he would receive me willingly and treat me well; and I answered, that I would gladly do so.

Clementia. And what good do you expect from this mad proceeding?

Lelia. The good of seeing him, hearing him, talking with him, learning his secrets, seeing his companions, and being sure that if he is not mine, he is not another's.

Clementia. In what way do you serve him?

Lelia. As his page, in all honesty. And in this fortnight that I have served him, I have become so much in favour, that I almost think appearing in my true dress would revive his love.

Clementia. What will people say when this shall be known?

Lelia. Who will know it, if you do not tell it? Now what I want you to do is this: that, as my father returned yesterday, and may perhaps send for me, you would prevent his doing so for four or five days, and at the end of that time I will return. You may say, that I have gone to Roverino with Sister Amabile.

Clementia. And why all this?

Lelia. Flaminio, as I have already told you, is enamoured of Isabella Foiani; and he often sends me to her with letters and messages. She, taking me for a young man, has fallen madly in love with me, and makes me the most passionate advances. I pretend that I will not love her, unless she can so manage as to bring Flaminio's pursuit of her to an end : and I hope that in three or four days he will be brought to give her up.

Clementia. Your father has sent me for you, and I insist on your coming to my house, and I will send for your clothes. If you do not come with me, I will tell your father all about you.

Lelia. Then I will go where neither you nor he shall ever see me again. I can say no more now, for I hear Flaminio call me. Expect me at your house in an hour. Remember, that I call myself Fabio degl' Alberini. I come, Signor. Adieu, Clementia.

Clementia (alone). In good faith, she has seen Gherardo coming, and has run away. I must not tell her father for the present, and she must not remain where she is. I will wait till I see her again.

SCENE IV.

GHERARDO, SPELA, *and* CLEMENTIA.

In this scene, CLEMENTIA makes sport of the old lover, treating him as a sprightly youth. He swallows the flattery, and echoes it in rapturous speeches, while his servant, Spela, in a series of asides, exhausts on his folly the whole vocabulary of anger and contempt.

SCENE V.

SPELA *and* SCATIZZA.

SPELA, at first alone, soliloquizes in ridicule of his master. Scatizza, the servant of Virginio, who had been to fetch Lelia from the convent, enters in great wrath, having been laughed at by the nuns, who told

him all sorts of contradictory stories respecting her;
by which he is so bewildered, that he does not know
what to say to Virginio.

ACT II.

SCENE I.—*The Street, with the house of Flaminio.*

LELIA (*as* FABIO) *and* FLAMINIO.

Flaminio. It is a strange thing, Fabio, that I have
not yet been able to extract a kind answer from this
cruel, this ungrateful Isabella, and yet her always
receiving you graciously, and giving you willing
audience, makes me think that she does not altogether
hate me.   Assuredly, I never did anything, that I
know, to displease her; and you may judge, from her
conversation, if she has any cause to complain of me.
Repeat to me what she said yesterday, when you
went to her with that letter.

Lelia. I have repeated it to you twenty times.

Flaminio. Oh repeat it to me once more.   What can
it matter to you?

Lelia. It matters to me this, that it is disagreeable
to you, and is, therefore, painful to me, as your servant, who seek only to please you ; and perhaps these
answers may give you ill-will towards me.

Flaminio. No, my dear Fabio; I love you as a
brother : I know you wish well to me, and I will
never be wanting to you, as time shall show.   But
repeat to me what she said.

Lelia. Have I not told you? That the greatest pleasure you can do her is to let her alone; to think no more of her, because she has fixed her heart elsewhere: that she has no eyes to look on you; that you lose your time in following her, and will find yourself at last with your hands full of wind.

Flaminio. And does it appear to you, Fabio, that she says these things from her heart, or, rather, that she has taken some offence with me? For at one time she showed me favour, and I cannot believe that she wishes me ill, while she accepts my letters and my messages. I am disposed to follow her till death. Do you not think me in the right, Fabio?

Lelia. No, signor.

Flaminio. Why?

Lelia. Because, if I were in your place, I should expect her to receive my service as a grace and an honour. To a young man like you, noble, virtuous, elegant, handsome, can ladies worthy of you be wanting? Do as I would do, sir: leave her; and attach yourself to some one who will love you as you deserve. Such will be easily found, and perhaps as handsome as she is. Have you never yet found one in this country who loved you?

Flaminio. Indeed I have, and especially one, who is named Lelia, and of whom, I have often thought, I see a striking likeness in you: the most beautiful, the most accomplished, the most courteous young person in this town: who would think herself happy, if I would show her even a little favour: rich, and well received at court. We were lovers nearly a year, and she showed me a thousand favours: but she went to Mirandola, and my fate made me

enamoured of Isabella, who has been as cruel to me
as Lelia was gracious.

Lelia. Master, you deserve to suffer. If you do
not value one who loves you, it is fitting that one
you love should not value you.

Flaminio. What do you mean?

Lelia. If you first loved this poor girl, and if she
loved and still loves you, why have you abandoned
her to follow another? Ah, Signor Flaminio! you
do a great wrong, a greater than I know if God can
pardon.

Flaminio. You are a child, Fabio. You do not
know the force of love. I cannot help myself. I
must love and adore Isabella. I cannot, may not,
will not think of any but her. Therefore, go to her
again: speak with her: and try to draw dextrously
from her, what is the cause that she will not see me.

Lelia. You will lose your time.

Flaminio. It pleases me so to lose it.

Lelia. You will do nothing.

Flaminio. Patience.

Lelia. Pray let her go.

Flaminio. I cannot. Go, as I bid you.

Lelia. I will go, but—

Flaminio. Return with the answer immediately.
Meanwhile I will go in.

Lelia. When time serves, I will not fail.

Flaminio. Do this, and it will be well for you.

SCENE II.

LELIA *and* PASQUELLA.

Lelia. He has gone in good time, for here is Pasquella coming to look for me.   [LELIA *retires.*

Pasquella. I do not think there is in the world a greater trouble, or a greater annoyance, than to serve a young woman like my mistress, who has neither mother nor sisters to look after her, and who has fallen all at once into such a passion of love, that she has no rest night or day, but runs about the house, now up stairs, now down, now to one window, now to another, as if she had quicksilver in her feet. Oh! I have been young, and I have been in love : but I gave myself some repose. At least, if she had fallen in love with a man of note, and of fitting years: but she has taken to doting on a boy, who, I think, could scarcely tie the points of his doublet, if he had not some one to help him : and every day, and all day, she sends me to look for him, as if I had nothing to do at home. But here he is, happily. Good day to you, Fabio. I was seeking you, my charmer.

Lelia. And a thousand crowns to you, Pasquella. How does your fair mistress?

Pasquella. And how can you suppose she does? Wastes away in tears and lamentations, that all this morning you have not been to her house.

Lelia. She would not have me there before daybreak. I have something to do at home. I have a master to serve.

Pasquella. Your master always wishes you to go

there : and my mistress entreats you to come, for her father is not at home, and she has something of consequence to tell you.

Lelia. Tell her she must get rid of Flaminio, or I shall ruin myself by obeying her.

Pasquella. Come, and tell her so yourself.

Lelia. I have something else to do, I tell you.

Pasquella. It is but to go, and return as soon as you please.

Lelia. I will not come. Go, and tell her so.

Pasquella. You will not?

Lelia. No, I say. Do you not hear? No. No. No.

Pasquella. In good faith, in good truth, Fabio, Fabio, you are too proud: you are young: you do not know your own good: this favour will not last always; you will not always have such rosy cheeks, such ruby lips: when your beard grows, you will not be the pretty pet you are now. Then you will repent your folly. How many are there in this city, that would think the love of Isabella the choicest gift of heaven!

Lelia. Then let her give it to them : and leave alone me, who do not care for it.

Pasquella. Oh, heaven! how true is it, that boys have no brains. Oh, dear, dear Fabio, pray come, and come soon, or she will send me for you again, and will not believe that I have delivered her message.

Lelia. Well, Pasquella, go home. I did but jest. I will come.

Pasquella. When, my jewel?

Lelia. Soon.

Pasquella. How soon?

Lelia. Immediately: go.

Pasquella. I shall expect you at the door.

Lelia. Yes, yes.

Pasquella. If you do not come, I shall be very angry.

SCENE III.—*A Street, with two hotels and the house of Gherardo.*

GIGLIO (*a Spaniard*) *and* PASQUELLA.

GIGLIO, who is in love with Isabella, and longs for an opportunity of speaking to her without witnesses, tries to cajole Pasquella into admitting him to the house,* and promises her a rosary, with which he is to return in the evening. She does not intend to admit him, but thinks to trick him out of the rosary. He does not intend to give her the rosary, but thinks to delude her by the promise of it.

SCENE IV.—*The Street, with the house of Flaminio.*

FLAMINIO, CRIVELLO, *and* SCATIZZA.

Flaminio. You have not been to look for Fabio, and he does not come. I do not know what to think of his delay.

Crivello. I was going, and you called me back. How am I to blame?

Flaminio. Go now, and if he is still in the house of Isabella, wait till he comes out, and send him home instantly.

* Por mia vida, que esta es la Vieia biene avventurada, que tiene la mas hermosa moza d' esta tierra per sua ama. O se le puodiesse io ablar dos parablas sin testiges. . . . . . Quiero veer se puode con alguna lisenia, pararme tal con esta vieia ellacca ob alcatieta que me aga al canzar alge con ella.

Crivello. How shall I know if he is there or not? You would not have me knock and inquire?

Flaminio. I have not a servant worth his salt, but Fabio. Heaven grant me favour to reward him. What are you muttering, blockhead? Is it not true?

Crivello. What would you have me say? Of course I say, yes. Fabio is good: Fabio is handsome: Fabio serves well: Fabio with you: Fabio with your lady: Fabio does everything: Fabio is everything. But—

Flaminio. What do you mean by but?

Crivello. He is too much trusted: he is a stranger, and one day he may disappear, with something worth taking.

Flaminio. I wish you others were as trustworthy. Yonder is Scatizza. Ask him if he has seen Fabio: and come to me at the bank of the Porini.

The scene terminates with a few words between Crivello and Scatizza.

SCENE V.— SPELA soliloquizes on the folly of Gherardo, who had sent him to buy a bottle of perfume; and some young men in the shop, understanding for whom it was wanted, had told him he had better buy a bottle of assafœtida.

SCENE VI.—*The street with the hotels and the house of Gherardo.*

CRIVELLO, SCATIZZA, LELIA, *and* ISABELLA.

CRIVELLO *and* SCATIZZA are talking of keeping Carnival at the expense of their masters, when Gherardo's door opens, and they stand back. Lelia and Isabella enter from the house of Gherardo.

Lelia. Remember what you have promised me.

Isabella. And do you remember to return to me. One word more.

Lelia. What more?

Isabella. Listen.

Lelia. I attend.

Isabella. No one is here.

Lelia. Not a living soul.

Isabella. Come nearer. I wish——

Lelia. What do you wish?

Isabella. I wish that you would return after dinner, when my father will be out.

Lelia. I will; but if my master passes this way, close the window, and retire.

Isabella. If I do not, may you never love me.

Lelia. Adieu. Now return into the house.

Isabella. I would have a favour from you.

Lelia. What?

Isabella. Come a little within.

Lelia. We shall be seen.

Scatizza (apart). She has kissed him.

Crivello (apart). I had rather have lost an hundred crowns than not have seen this kiss. What will my master do when he knows it?

Scatizza (apart). Oh, the devil! You won't tell him?

Isabella. Pardon me. Your too great beauty, and the too great love I bear you, have impelled me to this. You will think it scarcely becoming the modesty of a maid; but God knows, I could not resist.

Lelia. I need no excuses, signora. I know too well what extreme love has led me to.

Isabella. To what?

Lelia. To deceiving my master, which is not well.

Isabella. Ill fortune come to him.

Lelia. It is late. I must go home. Remain in peace.

Isabella. I give myself to you.

Lelia. I am yours. (*Isabella goes in.*) I am sorry for her, and wish I were well out of this intrigue. I will consult my nurse, Clementia; but here comes Flaminio.

Crivello (apart). Scatizza, my master told me to go to him at the bank of the Porini. I will carry him this good news. If he does not believe me, I shall call you to witness.

Scatizza. I will not fail you; but if you will take my advice, you will keep quiet, and you will always have this rod in pickle for Fabio, to make him do as you please.

Crivello. I tell you I hate him. He has ruined me.

Scatizza. Take your own way.

SCENE VII.—*The Street, with the house of Flaminio.*

FLAMINIO *and* LELIA.

Flaminio. Is it possible that I can be so far out of myself, have so little self-esteem, as to love, in her own despite, one who hates me, despises me, will not even condescend to look at me? Am I so vile, of so little account, that I cannot free myself from this shame, this torment? But here is Fabio. Well, what have you done?

Lelia. Nothing.

Flaminio. Why have you been so long away?

Lelia. I have delayed, because I waited to speak with Isabella.

Flaminio. And why have you not spoken to her?

Lelia. She would not listen to me; and if you would act in my way, you would take another course; for by all that I can so far understand, she is most obstinately resolved to do nothing to please you.

Flaminio. Why, even now, as I passed her house, she rose and disappeared from the window, with as much anger and fury as if she had seen some hideous and horrible thing.

Lelia. Let her go, I tell you. Is it possible that, in all this city, there is no other who merits your love as much as she does?

Flaminio. I would it were not so. I fear this has been the cause of all my misfortune; for I loved very warmly that Lelia Bellenzini, of whom I have spoken; and I fear Isabella thinks this love still lasts, and on that account will not see me; but I will give Isabella to understand, that I love Lelia no longer; rather that I hate her, and cannot bear to hear her named, and will pledge my faith never to go where she may be. Tell Isabella this as strongly as you can.

Lelia. Oh, me!

Flaminio. What has come over you? What do you feel?

Lelia. Oh, me!

Flaminio. Lean on me. Have you any pain?

Lelia. Suddenly. In the heart.

Flaminio. Go in. Apply warm cloths to your side. I will follow immediately, and, if necessary, will send for a doctor to feel your pulse and prescribe a remedy. Give me your arm. You are pale and cold. Lean on me. Gently—gently. (*Leads her into the house, and returns.*) To what are we subject! I would not, for all I am worth, that anything should happen to him, for there never was in the world a more diligent and well-mannered servant, nor one more cordially attached to his master. (*Flaminio goes off, and Lelia returns.*)

Lelia. Oh, wretched Lelia! Now you have heard from the mouth of this ungrateful Flaminio, how well he loves you. Why do you lose your time in following one so false and so cruel? All your former love, your favours, and your prayers, were thrown away. Now your stratagems are unavailing. Oh, me, unhappy! Refused, rejected, spurned, hated! Why do I serve him, who repels me? Why do I ask him, who denies me? Why do I follow him, who flies me? Why do I love him, who hates me? Ah, Flaminio! Nothing pleases him but Isabella. He desires nothing but Isabella. Let him have her. Let him hold her. I must leave him, or I shall die. I will serve him no longer in this dress. I will never again come in his way since he holds me in such deadly hatred. I will go to Clementia, who expects me, and with her I will determine on the course of my future life.

SCENE VIII.

FLAMINIO *and* CRIVELLO.

Crivello. And if it is not so, cut out my tongue, and hang me up by the neck.

Flaminio. How long since?

Crivello. When you sent me to look for him.

Flaminio. Tell me again how it was, for he denies having been able to speak with her.

Crivello. You will do well to make him confess it. I tell you, that, watching about the house to see if he were there, I saw him come out; and as he was going away, Isabella called him back into the doorway. They looked round, to see if any one were near, and not seeing any one, they kissed together.

Flaminio. How was it that they did not see you?

Crivello. I was ensconced in the opposite portico.

Flaminio. How then did you see them?

Crivello. By peeping in the nick of time, when they saw nothing but each other.

Flaminio. And he kissed her?

Crivello. I do not know whether he kissed her, or she kissed him; but I am sure that one kissed the other.

Flaminio. Be sure that you saw clearly, and do not come by-and-by to say that it seemed so; for this is a great matter that you tell me of. How did you see it?

Crivello. Watching with open eyes, and having nothing to do but to see.

Flaminio. If this be true, you have killed me.

Crivello. This is true. She called him back, she went up to him: she embraced him; she kissed him. If this is to kill you, you are dead.

Flaminio. It is no wonder that the traitor denied having been there. I know now, why he counselled me to give her up: that he might have her himself. If I do not take such vengeance, as shall be a warning to all traitorous servants, may I never be esteemed a man. But I will not believe you, without better evidence. You are ill-disposed to Fabio, and wish to get rid of him; but by the eternal heaven, I will make you tell the truth, or I will kill you. You saw them kissing?

Crivello. I did.

Flaminio. He kissed her?

Crivello. Or she him.   Or both.

Flaminio. How often?

Crivello. Twice.

Flaminio. Where?

Crivello. In the entry of her house.

Flaminio. You lie in your throat.   You said in the doorway.

Crivello. Just inside the doorway.

Flaminio. Tell the truth.

Crivello. I am very sorry to have told it.

Flaminio. It was true?

Crivello. Yes; and I have a witness.

Flaminio. Who?

Crivello. Virginio's man, Scatizza.

Flaminio. Did he see it?

Crivello. As I did.

Flaminio. And if he does not confess it?

Crivello. Kill me.

Flaminio. I will.

Crivello. And if he does confess it?

Flaminio. I will kill both.

Crivello. Oh the devil!   What for?

Flaminio. Not you.   Isabella and Fabio.

Crivello. And burn down the house, with Pasquella and every one in it.

Flaminio. Let us look for Scatizza. I will pay them. I will take such revenge, as all this land shall ring of.

ACT III.

SCENE I.—*The Street, with the hotels and the house of Gherardo.*

MESSER PIERO, FABRIZIO, *and* STRAGUALCIA.

Messer Piero, who had been before in Modena, points out some of its remarkable places to Fabrizio, who had been taken from it too young to remember it. Stragualcia is a hungry fellow, who is clamorous for his dinner.

SCENE II.

L' AGIATO, FRUELLA, PIERO, FABRIZIO, *and* STRAGUALCIA.

L' AGIATO and FRUELLA, two rival hotel-keepers, dispute the favour of the new comers.

L'Agiato. Oh, Signors, this is the hotel; lodge at the Looking-glass—at the Looking-glass.

Fruella. Welcome, Signors: I have lodged you before. Do you not remember your Fruella? The only hotel for gentlemen of your degree.

L'Agiato. You shall have good apartments, a good fire, excellent beds, white crisp sheets; everything you can ask for.

Fruella. I will give you the best wine of Lombardy: partridges, home-made sausages, pigeons, pullets; and whatever else you may desire.

L'Agiato. I will give you veal sweetbreads, Bologna sausages, Mountain wine, all sorts of delicate fare.

Fruella. I will give you fewer delicacies, and more substantials. You will live at a fixed rate. At the Looking-Glass, you will be charged even for candles.

Stragualcia. Master, let us put up here. This seems best.

L'Agiato. If you wish to live well, lodge at the Looking-Glass. You would not have it said that you lodged at the Fool.*

Fruella. My Fool is a hundred thousand times better than your Looking-Glass.

Messer Piero. *Speculum prudentiam significat, juxta illud nostri Catonis, Nosce teipsum.*† You understand, Fabrizio.

Fabrizio. I understand.

Fruella. See who has most guests, you or I.

L'Agiato. See who has most men of note.

Fruella. See where they are best treated.

L'Agiato. See where there are most delicacies.

Stragualcia. Delicacies, delicacies, delicacies! Give me substance. Delicacies are for the Florentines.

L'Agiato. All these lodge with me.

Fruella. They did ; but for the last three years they have come to me.

L'Agiato. My man, give me the trunk, it seems to gall your shoulder.

Stragualcia. Never mind my shoulder, I want to fill my stomach.

---

* In the sense of *fou*, not of *sot*.

† The looking-glass signifies prudence, according to the saying of our Cato : " Know yourself."

Fruella. Here is a couple of capons, just ready. These are for you.

Stragualcia. They will do for a first course.

L'Agiato. Look at this ham.

Messer Piero. Not bad.

Fruella. Who understands wine?

Stragualcia. I do; better than the French.

Fruella. See if this pleases you. If not, you may try ten other sorts.

Stragualcia. Fruella, you are the prince of hosts. Taste this, master. This is good. Carry in the trunk.

Messer Piero. Wait a little. What have you to say?

L'Agiato. I say, that gentlemen do not care for heavy meats, but for what is light, good, and delicate.

Stragualcia. This would be an excellent *provedore* for a hospital.

Messer Piero. Do not be uncivil. What will you give us?

L'Agiato. You have only to command.

Fruella. Where there is plenty, a man may eat little or much as he pleases; but where there is little, and the appetite grows with eating, he can only finish his dinner with bread.

Stragualcia. You are wiser than the statutes. I have never seen a landlord so much to my mind.

Fruella. Go into the kitchen, brother; there you will see.

Messer Piero. *Omnis repletio mala, panis autem pessima.**

---

* All repletion is bad, but that of bread is the worst.

Stragualcia (*aside*). Paltry pedant! One of these days I must crack his skull.

L'Agiato. Come in, gentlemen. It is not good to stand in the cold.

Fabrizio. We are not so chilly.

Fruella. You must know, gentlemen, this hotel of the Looking-Glass used to be the best hotel in Lombardy; but since I have opened this of the Fool, it does not lodge ten persons in a year, and my sign has a greater reputation throughout the world than any other hostelry whatever. The French come here in flocks, and all the Germans, that pass this way.

L'Agiato. That is not true. The Germans go to the Pig.

Fruella. The Milanese come here; the Parmesans, the Placentians.

L'Agiato. The Venetians come to me, the Genoese, the Florentines.

Messer Piero. Where do the Neapolitans lodge?

Fruella. With me.

L'Agiato. The greater part of them lodge at the Cupid.

Fruella. Many with me.

Fabrizio. Where does the Duke of Malfi?

Fruella. Sometimes at my house, sometimes at his, sometimes at the Sword, sometimes at the Cupid; accordingly as he finds most room for his suite.

Messer Piero. Where do the Romans lodge, as we are from Rome?

L'Agiato. With me.

Fruella. It is not true. He does not lodge a Roman in a year, except two or three old cardinals, who keep to him from habit. All the rest come to the Fool.

Stragualcia. I would not go from hence, without being dragged away. Master, there are so many pots and pipkins about the fire, so many soups, so many sauces, so many spits, turning with partridges and capons, such an odour of stews and ragouts, such a display of pies and tarts, that, if the whole court of Rome were coming here to keep carnival, there would be enough, and to spare.

Fabrizio. Have you been drinking?

Stragualcia. Oh! and such wine.

Messer Piero. *Variorum ciborum commistio pessimam generat digestionem.**

Stragualcia. *Rus asinorum, buorum castronorum pecoronibus* †—the devil take all pedants. Let us go in here, master.

Fabrizio. Where do the Spaniards lodge?

Fruella. I do not trouble myself about them. They go to the Hook. But what need more? No person of note arrives in Modena, but comes to lodge with me, except the Sienese, who, being all one with the Modenese, no sooner set foot in the city, but they find an hundred friends, who take them to their houses : otherwise great lords and good companions, gentle and simple, all come to the Fool.

L'Agiato. I say that great doctors, learned brothers, academicians, virtuosi, all come to the Looking-Glass.

Fruella. And I say, that no one, who takes up his

* The mixture of various foods causes the worst possible digestion.

† Mock Latin.

quarters at the Looking-Glass, has been there many days, before he walks out and comes to me.

Fabrizio. Messer Piero, what shall we do?

Messer Piero. *Etiam atque etiam cogitandum.**

Stragualcia (aside). I can scarcely keep my hands off him.

Messer Piero. I think, Fabrizio, we have not much money.

Stragualcia. Master, I have just seen the host's daughter, as beautiful as an angel.

Messer Piero. Well, let us fix here. Your father, if we find him, will pay the reckoning.

Stragualcia. I will go into the kitchen, taste what is there, drink two or three cups of wine, fall asleep by a good fire, and the devil take economy.

L'Agiato. Remember, Fruella. You have played me too many tricks. One day we must try which head is the hardest.

Fruella. Whenever you please. I am ready to crack your skull.

SCENE III.—*The Street, with the house of Virginio.*

VIRGINIO *and* CLEMENTIA.

Virginio. These are the customs which you have taught her. This is the honour which she does me. Have I for this escaped so many misfortunes, to see my property without an heir, my house broken up, my daughter dishonoured: to become the fable of the city: not to dare to lift up my head: to be pointed at by boys; to be laughed at by old men, to be put into a comedy by the Intronati, to be made an example in novels, to be an eternal scandal in

* It is to be thought of again and again.

the mouths of the ladies of this land? For if one knows it, in three hours all the city knows it. Disgraced, unhappy, miserable father! I have lived too long. What can I think of? What can I do?

Clementia. You will do well to make as little noise as you can, and to take the quietest steps you can to bring your daughter home, before the town is aware of the matter. But I wish that Sister Novellante Ciancini had as much breath in her body, as I have faith in my mind that Lelia goes dressed as a man. Do not encourage their evil speaking. They wish her to be a nun, that they may inherit your property.

Virginio. Sister Novellante has spoken truth. She has told me, moreover, that Lelia is living as a page with a gentleman of this city, and that he does not know that she is not a boy.

Clementia. I do not believe it.

Virginio. Neither do I, that he does not know that she is not a boy.

Clementia. That is not what I mean.

Virginio. It is what I mean. But what could I expect, when I intrusted her bringing up to you?

Clementia. Rather, what could you expect, when you wanted to marry her to a man old enough to be her grandfather?

Virginio. If I find her, I will drag her home by the hair.

Clementia. You will take your disgrace from your bosom, to display it on your head.

Virginio. I have a description of her dress: I shall find her: let that suffice.

Clementia. Take your own way. I will lose no more time in washing a coal.

SCENE IV.—*The Street, with the hotels and the house of Gherardo.*

FABRIZIO *and* FRUELLA.

Fabrizio. While my two servants are sleeping, I will walk about to see the city. When they rise, tell them to come towards the piazza.

Fruella. Assuredly, young gentleman, if I had not seen you put on these clothes, I should have taken you for the page of a gentleman in this town, who dresses like you, in white,* and is so like you that he appears yourself.

Fabrizio. Perhaps I may have a brother.

Fruella. It may be so.

Fabrizio. Tell my tutor to inquire for he knows whom.

Fruella. Trust to me.

SCENE V.

FABRIZIO *and* PASQUELLA.

Pasquella. In good faith, there he is. I was afraid of having to search the city before I should find you. My mistress says you must come to her as soon as you can, for a matter of great importance to both of you.

---

* Viola, in assuming male apparel, copies the dress of her brother :—

> "He named Sebastian : I my brother know
> Yet living in my glass : even such and so
> In favour was my brother; and he went
> Still in this fashion, colour, ornament;
> For him I imitate."—*Twelfth Night, Act* iii., *Scene* 4.

Fabrizio. Who is your mistress?

Pasquella. As if you did not know.

Fabrizio. I do not know either her or you.

Pasquella. Oh, my Fabio.

Fabrizio. That is not my name. You are under some mistake.

Pasquella. Oh, no, Fabio. You know, there are few girls in this country so rich and so beautiful, and I wish you would come to conclusions with her : for going backwards and forwards day after day, taking words and giving words only, sets folks talking, with no profit to you, and little honour to her.

Fabrizio (*aside*). What can this mean? Either the woman is mad, or she takes me for somebody else. But I will see what will come of it. Let us go, then.

Pasquella. Oh! I think I hear people in the house. Stop a moment. I will see if Isabella is alone, and will make a sign to you if the coast is clear.

Fabrizio. I will see the end of this mystery. Perhaps it is a scheme to get money of me : but I am, as it were, a pupil of the Spaniards, and am more likely to get a crown from them, than they are to get a carlin from me. I will stand aside a little, to see who goes into or out of the house, and judge what sort of lady she may be.

SCENE VI.

GHERARDO, VIRGINIO, *and* PASQUELLA.

Gherardo. Pardon me. If this is so, I renounce her. If Lelia has done this, it must be, not merely because she will not have me, but because she has taken somebody else.

Virginio. Do not believe it, Gherardo. I pray you, do not spoil what has been done.

Gherardo. And I pray you to say no more about it.

Virginio. Surely you will not be wanting to your word.

Gherardo. Yes, where there has been a wanting in deed. Besides, you do not know if you can recover her. You are selling the bird in the bush. I heard your talk with Clementia.

Virginio. If I do not recover her, I cannot give her to you. But if I do recover her, will you not have her? And that immediately?

Gherardo. Virginio, I had the most honourable wife in Modena. And I have a daughter who is a dove. How can I bring into my house one who has run away from her father, and gone heaven knows where, in masculine apparel? Whom should I find to marry my daughter?

Virginio. After a few days nothing will be thought of it. And I do not think any one knows it, except ourselves.

Gherardo. The whole town will be full of it.

Virginio. No, no.

Gherardo. How long is it since she ran away?

Virginio. Yesterday, or this morning.

Gherardo. Who knows that she is still in Modena?

Virginio. I know it.

Gherardo. Find her, and we will talk it over again.

Virginio. Do you promise to take her?

Gherardo. I will see.

Virginio. Say, yes.

Gherardo. I will not say yes : but—

Virginio. Come, say it freely.

Gherardo. Softly. What are you doing here, Pasquella? What is Isabella about?

Pasquella. Kneeling before her altar.

Gherardo. Blessings on her. A daughter who is always at her devotions, is something to be proud of.

Pasquella. Ay, indeed. She fasts on all fast-days, and says the prayers of the day like a little saint.

Gherardo. She resembles that blessed soul of her mother.

Virginio. Oh, Gherardo! Gherardo! this is she, of whom we have been speaking. She seems to be hiding or running away, for having seen me. Let us go up to her.

Gherardo. Take care not to mistake. Perhaps it is not she?

Virginio. Who would not know her? And have I not all the signs which Sister Novellante gave me?

Pasquella. Things are going ill. I will take myself off.

SCENE VII.

VIRGINIO, GHERARDO, *and* FABRIZIO.

Virginio. So, my fine miss, do you think this a befitting dress for you? This is the honour which you do to my house. This is the content you give to a poor old man. Would I had been dead before you were born, for you were only born to disgrace me : to bury me alive. And you, Gherardo, what say you of your betrothed? Is she not a credit to you?

Gherardo. She is no betrothed of mine.

Virginio. Impudent minx! What would become of you, if this good man should reject you for a wife?

But he overlooks your follies, and is willing to take you.

Gherardo. Softly, softly.

Virginio. Go indoors, hussy.

Fabrizio. Old man, have you no sons, friends, or relations in this city, whose duty it is to take care of you?

Virginio. What an answer! Why do you ask this?

Fabrizio. Because I wonder that, having so much need of a doctor, you are allowed to go about, when you ought to be locked up, and in a strait-waistcoat.

Virginio. You ought to be locked up, and shall be, if I do not kill you on the spot, as I have a mind to do.

Fabrizio. You insult me, because, perhaps, you think me a foreigner; but I am a Modenese, and of as good a family as you.

Virginio (*taking Gherardo aside*). Gherardo, take her into your house. Do not let her be seen in this fashion.

Gherardo. No, no; take her home.

Virginio. Listen a little, and keep an eye on her, that she does not run away. (*They talk apart.*)

Fabrizio. I have seen madmen before now, but such a madman as this old fellow I never saw going at large. What a comical insanity, to fancy that young men are girls! I would not for a thousand crowns have missed this drollery, to make a story for evenings in carnival. They are coming this way. I will humour their foolery, and see what will come of it.

Virginio. Come here.

Fabrizio. What do you want?

E

Virginio. You are a sad hussy.

Fabrizio. Do not be abusive : for I shall not stand it.

Virginio. Brazen face.

Fabrizio. Ho! ho! ho!

Gherardo. Let him speak. Do you not see that he is angry? Do as he bids.

Fabrizio. What is his anger to me? What is he to me, or you either?

Virginio. You will kill me before my time.

Fabrizio. It is high time to die, when you have fallen into dotage. You have lived too long already.

Gherardo. Do not speak so, dear daughter, dear sister.

Fabrizio. Here is a pretty pair of doves! both crazy with one conceit. Ha! ha! ha! ha!

Virginio. Do you laugh at me, impudence?

Fabrizio. How can I help laughing at you, brainless old goose?

Gherardo. I am afraid this poor girl has lost her wits.

Virginio. I thought so at first, when I saw with how little patience she received me. Pray take her into your house. I cannot take her to my own, without making myself the sight of the city.

Fabrizio. About what are these brothers of Melchisedech laying together the heads of their second babyhood?

Virginio. Let us coax her indoors; and as soon as she is within, lock her up in a chamber with your daughter.

Gherardo. Be it so.

Virginio. Come, my girl, I will not longer be angry with you. I pardon everything. Only behave well for the future.

Fabrizio. Thank you.

Gherardo. Behave as good daughters do.

Fabrizio. The other chimes in with the same tune.

Gherardo. Go in, then, like a good girl.

Virginio. Go in, my daughter.

Gherardo. This house is your own. You are to be my wife.

Fabrizio. Your wife and his daughter? Ha! ha! ha!

Gherardo. My daughter will be glad of your company,

Fabrizio. Your daughter, eh? Very good. I will go in.

Virginio. Gherardo, now that we have her safe, lock her up with your daughter, while I send for her clothes.

Gherardo. Pasquella, call Isabella, and bring the key of her room.

ACT IV.

SCENE I.—*Scene continues.*

MESSER PIERO *and* STRAGUALCIA.

Messer Piero. You ought to have fifty bastinadoes, to teach you to keep him company when he goes out, and not to get drunk and sleep, as you have done, and let him go about alone.

Stragualcia. And you ought to be loaded with birch and broom, sulphur, pitch, and gunpowder, and set on fire, to teach you not to be what you are.

Messer Piero. Sot, sot.

Stragualcia. Pedant, pedant.

Messer Piero. Let me find your master.

Stragualcia. Let me find his father.

Messer Piero. What can you say of me to his father?

Stragualcia. And what can you say of me?

Messer Piero. That you are a knave, a rogue, a rascal, a sluggard, a coward, a drunkard. That is what I can say.

Stragualcia. And I can say that you are a thief, a gambler, a slanderer, a cheat, a sharper, a boaster, a blockhead, an impostor, an ignoramus, a traitor, a profligate. That is what I can say.

Messer Piero. Well, we are both known.

Stragualcia. True.

Messer Piero. No more words. I will not place myself on a footing with you.

Stragualcia. Oh! to be sure; you have all the nobility of the Maremma. I am better born than you. What are you, but the son of a muleteer? This upstart, because he can say *cujus masculini*, thinks he may set his foot on every man's neck.

Messer Piero. Naked and poor go'st thou, Philosophy.* To what have poor letters come? Into the mouth of an ass.

Stragualcia. You will be the ass presently. I will lay a load of wood on your shoulders.

Messer Piero. *Furor fit læsa sæpius sapientia.†* For the sake of your own shoulders, let me alone, base groom, poltroon, arch-poltroon.

Stragualcia. Pedant, pedant, arch-pedant. What

---

* Povera e nuda vai, Filosofia.—*Petrarca*, p. 1. s. 7.

† Wisdom frequently injured becomes fury.

can be said worse than pedant? Can there be a viler, baser, more rubbishy race? They go about puffed up like bladders because they are called *Messer* This, *Maestro* That. . . . (*Stragualcia ends with several terms of untranslatable abuse.*)

Messer Piero. Tractant fabrilia fabri.* You speak like what you are. Either you shall leave this service, or I will.

Stragualcia. Who would have you in his house, and at his table, except my young master, who is better than bread?

Messer Piero. Many would be glad of me. No more words. Go to the hotel, take care of your master's property. By-and-by we will have a reckoning.

Stragualcia. Yes, we will have a reckoning, and you shall pay it.

Messer Piero. Fruella told me Fabrizio was gone towards the Piazza. I will follow him.　　　[*Exit.*

Stragualcia. If I did not now and then make head against this fellow, there would be no living with him. He has no more valour than a rabbit. When I brave him, he is soon silenced: but if I were once to knock under to him, he would lead me the life of a galley-slave.

SCENE II.

GHERARDO, VIRGINIO, *and* MESSER PIERO.

Gherardo. I will endow her as you desire; and if you do not find your son, you will add a thousand golden florins.

Virginio. Be it so.

---

* Workmen speak according to their art.

Messer Piero. I am much deceived, or I have seen this gentleman before.

Virginio. What are you looking at, good sir?

Messer Piero. Certainly, this is my old master. Do you know in this town one Signor Vincenzio Bellenzini?

Virginio. I know him well. He has no better friend than I am.

Messer Piero. Assuredly, you are he. *Salve, patronorum optime.**

Virginio. Are you Messer Pietro de' Pagliaricci, my son's tutor?

Messer Piero. I am, indeed.

Virginio. Oh, my son! Woe is me! What news do you bring me of him? Where did you leave him? Where did he die? For dead he must be, or I should not have been so long without hearing from him. Those traitors murdered him—those Jews, those dogs. Oh, my son! my greatest blessing in the world! Tell me of him, dear master.

Messer Piero. Do not weep, sir, for heaven's sake. Your son is alive and well.

Gherardo. If this is true, I lose the thousand florins. Take care, Virginio, that this man is not a cheat.

Messer Piero. *Parcius ista viris tamen objicienda memento.†*

Virginio. Tell me something, master.

Messer Piero. Your son, in the sack of Rome, was a prisoner of one Captain Orteca.

Gherardo. So he begins his fable.

* Hail! best of masters.

† Remember, that such things must be more sparingly objected to men.

Messer Piero. And because the captain had two comrades, who might claim their share, he sent us secretly to Siena: then, fearing that the Sienese, who are great friends of right and justice, and most affectionately attached to this city, might take him and set him at liberty, he took us to a castle of the Signor di Piombino, set our ransom at a thousand ducats, and made us write for that amount.

Virginio. Was my son ill-treated?

Messer Piero. No, certainly; they treated him like a gentleman.   We received no answers to our letters.

Virginio. Go on.

Messer Piero. Now, being conducted with the Spanish camp to Corregia, this captain was killed, and the Court took his property, and set us at liberty.

Virginio. And where is my son?

Messer Piero. Nearer than you suppose.

Virginio. In Modena.

Messer Piero. At the hotel of the Fool.

Gherardo. The thousand florins are gone; but it suffices to have her.   I am rich enough without them.

Virginio. I die with impatience to embrace him. Come, master.

Messer Piero. But what of Lelia?

Virginio. She has grown into a fine young woman. Has my son advanced in learning?

Messer Piero. He has not lost his time, *ut licuit per tot casus, per tot discrimina rerum.**

Virginio. Call him out. Say nothing to him.   Let me see if he will know me.

---

* As far as it was available, through so many accidents and disastrous chances.

Messer Piero. He went out a little while since.   I will see if he has returned.

SCENE III.

VIRGINIO, GHERARDO, MESSER PIERO, *and* STRAGUALCIA,
afterwards FRUELLA.

Messer Piero. Stragualcia, oh! Stragualcia, has Fabrizio returned?

Stragualcia. Not yet.

Messer Piero. Come here.   Speak to your old master. This is Signor Virginio.

Stragualcia. Has your anger passed away?

Messer Piero. You know I am never long angry with you.

Stragualcia. All's well, then.   Is this our master's father?

Messer Pietro. It is.

Stragualcia. Oh! worthy master.   You are just found in time to pay our bill at the Fool.

Messer Piero. This has been a good servant to your son.

Stragualcia. Has been only?

Messer Piero. And still is.

Virginio. I shall take care of all who have been faithful companions to my son.

Stragualcia. You can take care of me with little trouble.

Virginio. Demand.

Stragualcia. Settle me as a waiter with this host, who is the best companion in the world, the best provided, the most knowing, one that better understands the necessities of a foreign guest than any host I have ever seen. For my part, I do not think there is any other paradise on earth.

Gherardo. He has a reputation for treating well.

Virginio. Have you breakfasted?

Stragualcia. A little.

Virginio. What have you eaten?

Stragualcia. A brace of partridges, six thrushes, a capon, a little veal, with only two jugs of wine.*

Virginio. Fruella, give him whatever he wants, and leave the payment to me.

Stragualcia. Fruella, first bring a little wine for these gentlemen.

Messer Piero. They do not need it.

Stragualcia. They will not refuse. You must drink too, Master.

Messer Piero. To make peace with you, I am content.

Stragualcia. Signor Virginio, you have reason to thank the Master, who loves your son better than his own eyes.

Virginio. Heaven be bountiful to him.

Stragualcia. It concerns you first, and heaven after. Drink, gentleman.

Gherardo. Not now.

Stragualcia. Pray then, go in, till Fabrizio returns. And let us sup here this evening.

---

* The reader may be reminded of Massinger's *Justice Greedy* :—

" *Overreach.* Hungry again ! Did you not devour this morning A shield of brawn and a barrel of Colchester oysters ?

" *Greedy.* Why, that was, sir, only to scour my stomach— A kind of a preparative."

New Way to Pay Old Debts, Act iv., *Scene* 1.

Gherardo. I must leave you for a while. I have some business at home.

Virginio. Take care that Lelia does not get away.

Gherardo. That is what I am going for.

Virginio. She is yours. I give her to you. Arrange the matter to your mind.

SCENE IV.—*The Street, with the house of Virginio.*

GHERARDO, LELIA, *and* CLEMENTIA.

Gherardo. One cannot have all things one's own way. Patience. But how is this? Here is Lelia. That careless Pasquella has let her escape.

Lelia. Does it not appear to you, Clementia, that Fortune makes me her sport?

Clementia. Be of good cheer. I will find some means to content you. But come in, and change your dress. You must not be seen so.

Gherardo. I will salute her, however, and understand how she has got out. Good day to you, Lelia, my sweet spouse. Who opened the door to you? Pasquella, eh? I am glad you have gone to your nurse's house; but your being seen in this dress does little honour to you or to me.

Lelia. To whom are you speaking? What Lelia? I am not Lelia.

Gherardo. Oh! a little while ago, when your father and I locked you up with my daughter Isabella, did you not confess that you were Lelia? And now, you think I do not know you. Go, my dear wife, and change your dress.

Lelia. God send you as much of a wife, as I have fancy for you as a husband. (*Goes in.*)

Clementia. Go home, Gherardo. All women have their child's play,* some in one way, some in another. This is a very innocent one. Still these little amusements are not to be talked of.

Gherardo. No one shall know it from me. But how did she escape from my house, where I had locked her up with Isabella?

Clementia. Locked up whom?

Gherardo. Lelia; this Lelia.

Clementia. You are mistaken. She has not parted from me to-day; and for pastime she put on these clothes, as girls will do, and asked me if she did not look well in them?

Gherardo. You want to make me see double. I tell you I locked her up with Isabella.

Clementia. Whence come you now?

Gherardo. From the hotel of the Fool.

Clementia. Did you drink?

Gherardo. A little.

Clementia. Now go to bed, and sleep it off.

Gherardo. Let me see Lelia for a moment before I go, that I may give her a piece of good news.

Clementia. What news?

Gherardo. Her brother has returned safe and sound, and her father is waiting for him at the hotel.

Clementia. Fabrizio?

Gherardo. Fabrizio.

Clementia. I hasten to tell her.

Gherardo. And I to blow up Pasquella, for letting her escape.

---

* *Cittolezze ('zitellezze*), equivalent to *fanciullaggini.*

SCENE V.—*The Street, with the hotels and the house of Gherardo.*

PASQUELLA, *alone.*

PASQUELLA, who had only known Lelia as Fabio, and did not know what the two old men had meant, by calling the supposed Lelia, whom they had delivered to her charge, a girl, has nevertheless obeyed orders, in locking up Fabrizio with Isabella, and now in an untranslatable soliloquy, narrates, that the two captives had contracted matrimony by their own ritual.

SCENE VI.

PASQUELLA *and* GIGLIO.

PASQUELLA, seeing GIGLIO coming, retires within the court-yard, through the grated door of which the dialogue is carried on. Giglio wishes to obtain admission to Gherardo's house, without giving Pasquella the rosary he had promised her. He shows it to her, and withholds giving it, on pretence that it wants repairs. She, on the other hand, wishes to get the rosary, and give him nothing in return. She pretends to doubt if it is a true rosary, and prevails on him to let her count the beads. She then cries out, that the fowls are loose, and that she cannot open the door till she has got them in. Giglio declares that he sees no fowls; that she is imposing on him. She laughs at him: he expostulates, implores, threatens to break down the door, to set fire to the house, to burn everything in it, herself included. In the midst of his wrath, he sees Gherardo approaching, and runs away.

SCENE VII.

PASQUELLA and GHERARDO.

Gherardo. What were you doing at the gate, with that Spaniard ?

Pasquella. He was making a great noise about a rosary. I could not make out what he wanted.

Gherardo. Oh ! you have executed your trust well. I could find in my heart to break your bones.

Pasquella. For what ?

Gherardo. Because you have let Lelia escape. I told you to keep her locked in.

Pasquella. She is locked in.

Gherardo. I admire your impudence. She is not.

Pasquella. I say she is.

Gherardo. I have just left her with her nurse Clementia.

Pasquella. And I have just left her, where you ordered her to be kept.

Gherardo. Perhaps she came back before me.

Pasquella. She never went away. The chamber has been kept locked.

Gherardo. Where is the key ?

Pasquella. Here it is.

Gherardo. Give it me. If she is not there you shall pay for it.

Pasquella. And if she is there will you pay for it?

Gherardo. I will. You shall have a handsome present.

SCENE VIII.

PASQUELLA, FLAMINIO; *afterwards* GHERARDO.

Flaminio. Pasquella, how long is it since my Fabio was here ?

Pasquella. Why ?

Flaminio. Because he is a traitor, and I will punish him ; and because Isabella has left me for him. Fine honour to a lady of her position, to fall in love with a page.

Pasquella. Oh, do not say so. All the favours she has shown him are only for love of you.

Flaminio. Tell her she will repent ; and as for him, I carry this dagger for him.

Pasquella. While the dog barks, the wolf feeds.

Flaminio. You will see.   [*Exit.*

Gherardo. Oh me! to what have I come! oh traitor, Virginio! oh heaven! what shall I do?

Pasquella. What is the matter, master?

Gherardo. What is he that is with my daughter?

Pasquella. He? Why you told me, it was Virginio's daughter.

GHERARDO has discovered the clandestine marriage, and gives vent to his rage in untranslatable terms.

SCENE IX.

GHERARDO, VIRGINIO, *and* MESSER PIERO.

Messer Piero. I wonder he has not returned to the hotel. I do not know what to think of it.

Gherardo. Ho! ho! Virginio! this is a pretty outrage that you have put on me. Do you think I shall submit to it?

Virginio. What are you roaring about?

Gherardo. Do you take me for a sheep, you cheat, you thief, you traitor? But the governor shall hear of it.

Virginio. Have you lost your senses? Or, what is the matter?

Gherardo. Robber.

Virginio. I have too much patience.

Gherardo. Liar.

Virginio. You lie in your own throat.

Gherardo. Forger.

Messer Piero. Ah, gentlemen! what madness is this?

Gherardo. Let me come at him.

Messer Piero. What is between this gentleman and you?

Virginio. He wanted to marry my daughter, and I left her in his charge. I am afraid he has abused my confidence, and invents a pretext for breaking off.

Gherardo. The villain has ruined me. I will cut him to pieces.　　　　-　[*Virginio goes off.**

Messer Piero. Pray let us understand the case.

Gherardo. The miscreant has run away. Come in with me, and you shall know the whole affair.

Messer Piero. I go in with you, on your faith?

Gherardo. On my faith, solemnly.

* To return with arms and followers.

ACT V.

SCENE I.—*Scene continues.*

VIRGINIO, STRAGUALCIA, SCATIZZA ; *afterwards at inter-vals*, MESSER PIERO, GHERARDO, *and* FABRIZIO.

Virginio. Follow me, all ; and you, Stragualcia.

Stragualcia. With or without arms ? I have no arms.

Virginio. Take in the hotel something that will serve. I fear this madman may have killed my poor daughter.

Stragualcia. This spit is a good weapon. I will run him through and all his followers, like so many thrushes.

Scatizza. What are these flasks for ?

Stragualcia. To refresh the soldiers, if they should fall back in the first skirmish.

Virginio. The door opens. They have laid some ambuscade.

Messer Piero. Leave me to settle the matter, Signor Gherardo.

Stralgualcia. See, master, the tutor has rebelled, and sides with the enemy. There is no faith in this class of fellows. Shall I spit him first, and count one.

Messer Piero. Why these arms, my master ?

Virginio. What has become of my daughter ?

Messer Piero. I have found Fabrizio.

Virginio. Where ?

Messer Piero. Here, within. And he has taken a beautiful wife.

Virginio. A wife ?   And who ?

Messer Piero. The daughter of Gherardo.

Virginio. Gherardo !   It was but now he wanted to kill me.

*Messer Piero. Rem omnem a principio audies.** Come forth, Signor Gherardo.

Gherardo. Lay down these arms, and come in.   It is matter for laughter.

Virginio. Can I do it safely ?

Messer Piero. Safely, on my assurance.

Virginio. Then do you all go home, and lay down your arms.

Messer Piero. Fabrizio, come to your father.

Virginio. Is not this Lelia ?

Messer Piero. No, this is Fabrizio.

Virginio. Oh, my son, how much I have mourned for you ?

Fabrizio. Oh, dear father, so long desired !

Gherardo. Come in, and you shall know all.   I can further tell you, that your daughter is in the house of her nurse, Clementia.

Virginio. How thankful I am to Heaven.

SCENE II.—*The Street, with the houses of Virginio and Clementia.*

FLAMINIO *and* CRIVELLO ; *afterwards* CLEMENTIA.

Crivello. I have seen him in the house of Clementia with these eyes, and heard him with these ears.

Flaminio. Are you sure it was Fabio ?

Crivello. Do you think I do not know him ?

Flaminio. Let us go in, and if I find him——

---

* You shall hear the whole affair from the beginning.

Crivello. You will spoil all. Have patience, till he comes out.

Flaminio. Not heaven itself could make me have patience. (*Knocks at the door.*)

Clementia. Who is there?

Flaminio. A friend. Come down for a while.

Clementia. Oh, Signor Flaminio, what do you want with me?

Flaminio. Open, and I will tell you.

Clementia. Wait till I come down.

Flaminio. As soon as she opens the door, go in, and if you find him, call me.

Crivello. Leave it to me.

Clementia. Now what have you to say, Signor Flaminio?

Flaminio. What are you doing in your house with my page?

Clementia. What page? How? Are you going into my house by force? (*Pushing back Crivello.*)

Flaminio. Clementia, by the body of Bacchus! if you do not restore him ——

Clementia. Whom?

Flaminio. My boy, who has fled into your house.

Clementia. There is no boy in my house.

Flaminio. Clementia, you have always been friendly to me, and I to you; but this is a matter of too great moment——

Clementia. What fury is this? Pause a little, Flaminio. Give time for your anger to pass away.

Flaminio. I say, restore me Fabio.

Clementia. Oh! not so much rage. By my faith, if I were a young woman, and pleased you, I would have nothing to say to you. What of Isabella?

Flaminio. I wish she were quartered.

Clementia. Oh, that cannot be true.

Flaminio. If that is not true, she has made me see what is true.

Clementia. You young men deserve all the ill that can befall you. You are the most ungrateful creatures on earth.

Flaminio. This cannot be said of me. No man more abhors ingratitude than I do.

Clementia. I do not say it for you; but there is in this city a young woman, who, thinking herself beloved by a cavalier of your condition, became so much in love with him, that she seemed to see nothing in the world but him.

Flaminio. He was a happy man to inspire such a passion.

Clementia. It so happened that her father sent this poor girl away from Modena, and most bitterly she wept on her departure, fearing that he would soon forget her, and turn to another; which he did immediately.

Flaminio. This could not be a cavalier. He was a traitor.

Clementia. Listen. Worse follows. The poor girl, returning after a few months, and finding that her lover loved another, and that this other did not return his love, abandoned her home, placed her honour in peril, and, in masculine attire, engaged herself to her false lover as a servant.

Flaminio. Did this happen in Modena? I had rather be this fortunate lover than lord of Milan.

Clementia. And this lover, not knowing her, em-

ployed her as a messenger to his new flame, and she,
to please him, submitted to this painful duty.

Flaminio. Oh! virtuous damsel; oh! firm love: a
thing truly to be put in example to all coming time.
Oh! that such a chance had happened to me.

Clementia. You would not leave Isabella!

Flaminio. I would leave her, or any one thing else,
for such a blessing. Tell me, who is she?

Clementia. Tell me, first, what would you do, if the
case were your own?

Flaminio. I swear to you, by the light of heaven,
may I never more hold up my head among honourable men, if I would not rather take her for a wife,
even if she had no beauty, nor wealth, nor birth, than
the daughter of the Duke of Ferrara.

Clementia. This you swear.

Flaminio. This I swear, and this I would do.

Clementia. You are witness.

Crivello. I am.

Clementia. Fabio, come down.

SCENE III.

CLEMENTIA, FLAMINIO, CRIVELLO, LELIA *in female dress,
afterwards* PASQUELLA.

Clementia. This, Signor Flaminio, is your Fabio;
and this, at the same time, is the constant, loving girl
of whom I told you. Do you recognize him? Do you
recognize her? Do you now see the worth of the love
which you rejected?

Flaminio. There cannot be on earth a more charming

deceit than this. Is it possible, that I can have been so blind as not to have known her?

Pasquella. Clementia, Virginio desires that you will come to our house. He has given a wife to his son Fabrizio, who has just returned, and you are wanted to put everything in order.

Clementia. A wife? and whom?

Pasquella. Isabella, the daughter of my master Gherardo.

Flaminio. The daughter of Gherardo Foiani?

Pasquella. The same. I saw the ring put on the bride's finger.

Flaminio. When was this?

Pasquella. Just now. And I was sent off immediately to call Clementia.

Clementia. Say, I will come almost directly.

Lelia. Oh, heaven! all this together is enough to make me die of joy.

Pasquella. And I was to ask, if Lelia is here. Gherardo has said she is.

Clementia. Yes; and they want to marry her to the old phantom of your master, who ought to be ashamed of himself.

Flaminio. Marry her to Gherardo!

Clementia. See, if the poor girl is unfortunate.

Flaminio. May he have as much of life as he will have of her. I think, Clementia, this is certainly the will of heaven, which has had pity no less on this virtuous girl than on me; and therefore, Lelia, I desire no other wife than you, and I vow to you most solemnly, that if I have not you, I will never have any.

Lelia. Flaminio, you are my lord. I have shown my heart in what I have done.

Flaminio. You have, indeed, shown it well. And forgive me if I have caused you affliction; for I am most repentant, and aware of my error.

Lelia. Your pleasure, Flaminio, has always been mine. I should have found my own happiness in promoting yours.

Flaminio. Clementia, I dread some accident. I would not lose time, but marry her instantly, if she is content.

Lelia. Most content.

Clementia. Marry, then, and return here. In the mean time, I will inform Virginio, and wish bad night to Gherardo.

SCENE IV.—*The Street, with the hotels and the house of Gherardo.*

PASQUELLA *and* GIGLIO.

PASQUELLA again befools the Spaniard, who goes off, vowing that this is the last time she shall impose on him.

SCENE V.—*The Street, with the houses of Virginio and Clementia.*

Cittina.

FLAMINIO and LELIA have been married, and have returned to Clementia's house. CITTINA comes out from it, and delivers an untranslatable soliloquy.

SCENE VI.—*The Street, with the hotels and the house of Gherardo.*

ISABELLA *and* FABRIZIO, *afterwards* CLEMENTIA.

Isabella. I most certainly thought that you were the page of a gentleman of this city. He resembles you so much, that he must surely be your brother.

Fabrizio. I have been mistaken for another more than once to-day.

Isabella. Here is your nurse, Clementia.

Clementia. This must be he who is so like Lelia. Oh! my dear child, Fabrizio, how is it with you?

Fabrizio. All well, my dear nurse. And how is it with Lelia?

Clementia. Well, well; but come in. I have much to say to you all.

SCENE VII.

VIRGINIO *and* CLEMENTIA.

Virginio. I am so delighted to have recovered my son, that I am content with everything.

Clementia. It was the will of heaven that she should not be married to that withered old stick, Gherardo. But let us go into the hotel,* and complete our preparations. (*They go into the hotel.*)

STRAGUALCIA.

Spectators, do not expect that any of these characters will reappear. If you will come to supper

* It would seem that the nuptial feast is to be held at the Fool. Stragualcia had previously said, "Let us sup here this evening."—*Act* iv., *Scene* 3.

with us, I will expect you at the Fool; but bring money, for there entertainment is not gratis. If you will not come (and you seem to say 'No!'), show us that you have been satisfied here; and you, Intronati, give signs of rejoicing.

AELIA LAELIA CRISPIS:

AN ATTEMPT TO SOLVE THE AENIGMA.

AELIA LAELIA CRISPIS.

MANY learned men have offered explanations of this aenigma. None of these explanations have been found satisfactory. If that which I have to offer should meet with acceptance, it will appear that my erudite predecessors have overlooked the obvious in seeking for the recondite.

About two hundred years ago, a marble was found near Bologna, with the following inscription :—

D. M.

AELIA . LAELIA . CRISPIS .

NEC . VIR . NEC . MULIER . NEC . ANDROGYNA .

NEC . PUELLA . NEC . JUVENIS . NEC . ANUS .

NEC . CASTA . NEC . MERETRIX . NEC . PUDICA .

SED . OMNIA .

SUBLATA .

NEQUE . FAME . NEQUE . FERRO . NEQUE . VENENO .

SED . OMNIBUS .

NEC . COELO . NEC . AQUIS . NEC . TERRIS .

SED . UBIQUE . JACET .

LUCIUS . AGATHO . PRISCUS .

NEC . MARITUS . NEC . AMATOR . NEC NECESSARIUS .

NEQUE . MOERENS . NEQUE . GAUDENS . NEQUE . FLENS .

HANC . NEC . MOLEM . NEC . PYRAMIDEM .

NEC . SEPULCHRUM .

SED . OMNIA .

SCIT . ET . NESCIT .

CUI . POSUERIT .

TO THE GODS OF THE DEAD.

Aelia Laelia Crispis,
Not man, nor woman, nor hermaphrodite :
Not girl, nor youth, nor old woman :
Not chaste, nor unchaste, nor modest :
But all :
Carried off,
Not by hunger, nor by sword, nor by poison :
But by all :
Lies,
Not in air, not in earth, not in the waters :
But everywhere.
Lucius Agatho Priscus,
Not her husband, nor her lover, nor her friend :
Not sorrowing, nor rejoicing, nor weeping :
Erecting
This, not a stone-pile, nor a pyramid,
Nor a sepulchre :
But all :
Knows, and knows not,
To whom he erects it.

I believe this aenigma to consist entirely in the
contrast, between the general and particular consideration of the human body, and its accidents of
death and burial. Abstracting from it all but what
is common to all human bodies, it has neither age
nor sex ; it has no morals, good or bad : it dies from
no specific cause : lies in no specific place : is the
subject of neither joy nor grief to the survivor, who
superintends its funeral: has no specific monument
erected over it; is, in short, the abstraction con-
templated in the one formula : " Man that is born of
a woman ;" which the priest pronounces equally over
the new-born babe, the mature man or woman, and
the oldest of the old.

But considered in particular, that is, distinctively and individually, we see, in succession, man and woman, young and old, good and bad ; we see some buried in earth, some in sea, some in polar ice, some in mountain snow. We see a funeral superintended, here by one who rejoices, there by one who mourns ; we see tombs of every variety of form. The abstract superintendent of a funeral, abstractedly interring an abstract body, does not know to whom he raises the abstract monument, nor what is its form ; but the particular superintendent of a particular funeral knows what the particular monument is, and to whose memory it is raised.

So far the inscription on the marble found at Bologna. Another copy, in an ancient MS. at Milan, adds three lines, which do not appear to me to belong to the original inscription :—

> Hoc est sepulchrum, cadaver intus non·habens :
> Hoc est cadaver, sepulchrum extra non habens :
> Sed idem cadaver est et sepulchrum sibi.

> This is a sepulchre, not having a corpse within :
> This is a corpse, not having a sepulchre without :
> But the same is to itself both corpse and sepulchre.

These lines are the translation of a Greek epigram on Niobe : to whom they are strictly appropriate, and to whom I am contented to leave them :—

> Ὁ τύμβος οὗτος ἔνδον οὐκ ἔχει νεκρόν ·
> Ὁ νεκρὸς οὗτος ἐκτὸς οὐκ ἔχει τάφον ·
> Ἀλλ' αὐτὸς αὐτοῦ νεκρός ἐστι καὶ τάφος.
> —*Anthologia Palatina*, vii., 311.

There is another consideration, which makes the Milanese manuscript of more questionable authority than the Bolognese marble. The marble has the superscription, D.M. *Diis Manibus*: *To the Gods of the Dead*: which is suitable to the dead in all points of view, general and particular. The MS. has Am. P. P. D., *Amicus Propriâ Pecuniâ Dicavit*: *A friend has dedicated this monument at his own expense*: which is suitable only to a particular tomb, and a definite relation between the dead and the living.

THE END.